D0538774

BRANCH
RECEIVED
JAN 27 2016

NO LONGER PROPERTY OF
SEATTLE PUBLIC LIBRARY

ELLA AND PENGUIN
STICK TOGETHER

By Megan Maynor

Illustrated by Rosalinde Bonnet

HARPER

An Imprint of HarperCollinsPublishers

"Penguin, look what I got!" said Ella.

"Ooh, stickers!" Penguin bounced and clapped. "Can I have a star?

Can I have a moon?

Can I have a comet?"

"Yes, but these are not ordinary stickers," said Ella.

"They're not?"

"Are they smelly?"

"Can you eat them?"

"Do they talk?
Hello, sticker?"

"No," Ella whispered.
"They glow in the dark."
"Yikes!" Penguin yelped.

Ella and Penguin
stood in front of
the closet.

Ella leaned in. "The dark is so . . . *dark.*"
Penguin held on tight to Ella. "Maybe
the stickers will glow somewhere else—
somewhere *mostly* dark."

"Good idea," said Ella.
"Let's try it."

Phew!

So Ella and Penguin climbed into the bathtub
and closed the shower curtain.

"No glow."

They flipped over a laundry basket
and hid beneath it.

"Nope."

They opened two umbrellas
and ducked under them.

"Not dark enough."

Ella and Penguin stood in front of the closet again.
"Maybe the stickers will glow if we close the door
just a little bit," said Ella.

Ella baby-stepped into the closet.
"Okay, Penguin, come on in."

Penguin chewed his flipper. "Are there any spiders in there?"
"No," said Ella.

"Big dogs?"
"Uh-uh."

"Narwhals?"

Ella looked around.
"This closet is narwhal-free."

"Okay. . . ."
Penguin stepped in. He closed the door a tiny bit.

"How's that?"

"A little more," said Ella.

"A little more. . . ."

"Wait!" whispered Ella.
"Did you feel that?"
    "Feel what?" asked Penguin.
    "I don't know!"

" *AAAAH!*"

Ella and Penguin tumbled out
of the closet.

"Oh," said Ella.
"It was a scarf."

Ella and Penguin sat in front of the closet. "We have to go all the way into the dark," said Ella. "I think we can do it."

"We cannot do it," said Penguin.

"Don't you want to see the stickers glow?" asked Ella.
"Yes," said Penguin. "But I want to see them glow in the *light*."

"What if we hold hands?" asked Ella.

Penguin waddled from foot to foot.
He took a big breath and puffed out his cheeks.

Ella waited.

"Okay." Penguin held
out his flipper. "But!
Do. Not. Let. Go."
    "Never," said Ella.

Ella and Penguin
stepped into the closet.
Ella closed the door.
All the way.

"Ohhh . . . ," said Ella.

"Yeah. Too bad," said Penguin.

"The stickers are broken. Let's go."

"Penguin?"

"Yes."

"Are your eyes closed?"

"Yes."

"Open your eyes."

"Oh!" Penguin gasped.

"You know, I kind of like the dark
with all this glowing," said Penguin.

"Me too," said Ella.

"We could stay in here and play astronauts.

Or space pirates.

Or superspy cupcake chefs on Mars!"

Or how about this. I'm a penguin. And you're a girl. And we're friends— in space!"

Ella squeezed Penguin's flipper. "Perfect."

For Chloe, Emmett, and Willa
—M.M.

For Tess
—R.B.

Ella and Penguin Stick Together
Text copyright © 2016 by Megan Maynor
Illustrations copyright © 2016 by Rosalinde Bonnet
All rights reserved. Manufactured in China.
No part of this book may be used or reproduced in any manner whatsoever without written
permission except in the case of brief quotations embodied in critical articles and reviews.
For information address HarperCollins Children's Books, a division of HarperCollins Publishers,
195 Broadway, New York, NY 10007.
www.harpercollinschildrens.com

Library of Congress Cataloging-in-Publication Data

Maynor, Megan, author.
    Ella and Penguin Stick Together / by Megan Maynor ; illustrated by Rosalinde Bonnet. — First edition.
         pages cm
    Summary: Ella and Penguin want to see her new stickers glow in the dark, but neither of them
wants to go into a dark place.
    ISBN 978-0-06-233088-8 (hardcover)
    [1. Fear of the dark—Fiction. 2. Best friends—Fiction. 3. Friendship—Fiction. 4. Penguins—Fiction.
5. Humorous stories.] I. Bonnet, Rosalinde, illustrator. II. Title.
PZ7.1.M388Ell 2016   2014041210
[E]—dc23   CIP
                                                                    AC

The images for this book were created with watercolor and pencil on Hot Press, High White
watercolor paper, 200 lb., Saunders Waterford, and finalized in Adobe Photoshop.
Typography by Martha Rago
15 16 17 18 19 SCP 10 9 8 7 6 5 4 3 2 1
❖
First Edition